Fall O Ween Coloring Book For Adults

© 2024 Luka Poe

All rights reserved. No part of this publication may be reproduced, distributed, or transmitted in any form or by any means, including photocopying, recording, or any other electronic or mechanical method, without the prior written permission of the author or the publisher.